Fear nothing, Phineas Basil, for you, my son, have the strength of ten men!

Jen, Mom and Dad, Ben and Dive Team Alpha, Becky and Rachael, Karen Lotz, Ann and Kate, Neil and Aps, Capt. Crusty, and Dicky Gildenmeister—you kept your necks out all the way.

Copyright © 2008 by Timothy Basil Ering

First edition 2008

Library of Congress Cataloging-in-Publication Data

Ering, Timothy B.
Necks out for adventure! : the true story of Edwin Wiggleskin / Timothy Basil Ering — 1st ed.
p.   cm.
Summary: Unlike the other wiggleskins, who live happily in the mud and only stick their necks out to eat, Edwin is eager for different experiences and follows his mother's advice to stick his neck out for adventure.
ISBN 978-0-7636-2355-5
(1. Individuality—Fiction. 2. Self-confidence—Fiction. 3. Adventure and adventurers—Fiction.)
I. Title
PZ7.E725913Nec 2007
(E)—dc22 2006051854
10 9 8 7 6 5 4 3 2

Printed in China

This book was typeset in Tim Ering.
The illustrations were done in acrylic and ink on paper.

Candlewick Press
2067 Massachusetts Avenue
Cambridge, Massachusetts 02140

visit us at www.candlewick.com

Necks Out for Adventure!

The True Story of Edwin Wiggleskin

TIMOTHY BASIL ERING

Candlewick Press
Cambridge, Massachusetts

For as long as anyone could remember, the wiggleskins would not leave the mud.

While the currents flowed back and forth over their heads, they all lived by a simple system: Necks out to eat and...

necks in to hide.

That's how it always was, until one day when a young wiggleskin named Edwin asked his mom a very big question.

"What would happen if we flowed with the current?"

The other wiggleskins laughed, but Edwin's mom held him close. "Don't let them bother you, Son," she answered. "Stick your neck out for adventure like you always do."

But before Edwin could reply, a dark shadow fell across the wiggleskin bed. All the wiggleskins fell silent as the mud trembled, then suddenly...

two huge filthy feet appeared—and worse yet,
a terrible smell you'd never forget!

"Necks in to hide!" the wiggleskins all screeched.

But sadly, it was too late to hide.
Soon all the wiggleskins were gone.

All except one.

Why was Edwin left behind? No one knows.

Edwin's neck was pulled way in. He was dreadfully afraid.

Long, lonely hours passed, but no one returned. As Edwin waited and waited, he felt the current steadily push against him, encouraging him to search for the others.

"I can't move," he told the current. "I'm stuck in my shell."

And that, my friends, is when Edwin thought of his mom's last words to him: "Necks out for adventure."

So Edwin gathered up every bit of courage he had. With no one around to witness this unheard-of event, he pushed at both sides of his shell and—oh boy—

Edwin's skin wiggled as the water gently lifted him up and carried him away.

"Mom? Dad?" Edwin called out as he drifted over the seafloor. "Anybody?"

He floated along with magnificent squid-bellied lice, glimmering golden-eyed sliverstones, and a red-spotted scrintalberry leaf.

But then, without warning, the force from a tremendous wave sucked Edwin's belly up over his neck.

Up, up, up Edwin went!

SPOO-LASH!

The big wave spit Edwin from the sea onto the land.

For the first time ever, Edwin's toes touched dry sand.

"Where am I?" Edwin asked the wave. But the wave didn't answer. It just kept curling and breaking on the shore.

So Edwin began to walk. He walked until he could not take one more step under the scorching hot sun.

Completely exhausted and delirious from the heat,
Edwin flopped over face-first.

But then, as if in a scary dream, he smelled a smell,
that same terrible smell, the one he'd never forget!

Alas! Edwin saw the truth! The stink came from a hideous hornly scratcher, a wiggleskin's worst nightmare!

"Well, well, yes indeed.
A scrintalberry leaf, just what I need."

With one swipe of his giant toe, the scratcher flicked the scrintalberry leaf—and Edwin—into his moldy sack.

The stinky creature skipped off, whistling and singing to himself while Edwin flipped and jostled inside the sack.

"Scrintalberry leaves, my favorite spice,
   will season up my meal scrumptiously nice."

Then, without warning...

Edwin fell neck-first into a cooking pot
full of eel skins, fish butter, and squid broth!

"Kk-k-k-kkkkrrrrrrrr... k-k-kkrrrrrrr..." went the sharpening wheel.
And the scratcher sang a horrible little song.

"Wiggleskins, wiggleskins, so tender and sweet,
fresh boiled wiggleskins, my favorite treat."

Edwin screamed!

The scratcher snatched Edwin from the pot.

"Well, well, what do we have here in my stew?
It's a delicious wiggleskin, already shucked,
out of the blue."

Edwin didn't know how he'd thought
of it, but suddenly he had a plan.
He stretched out his neck and...

squirted that nasty old hornly scratcher right
in the eye! And hornly scratchers hate,

HATE,

HATE to be squirted in the eye!

The scratcher fell back, flipping his pot of stew into the air. Edwin quickly scurried for freedom. He dashed straight outside, off the step, around the corner of the shack, and, oh my, you'll never guess what stood in front of him this time!

It was a rusted, lonely cage, packed full of weeping wiggleskins.

"MOM!" Edwin shouted. "DAD!"

"EDWIN!" they cried.

"Necks out, everybody!" Edwin exclaimed.
"The hornly scratcher will be here any second
to gobble us all up!"

The wiggleskins realized what they had to do,
and, one by one, they shucked their shells, too.

"To the shore!" Edwin commanded. "Run like you've never run before!" (Which, in fact, none of them ever had.)

Although they were very dry and thirsty, the wiggleskins ran like the dickens, and a glorious thing happened as they ran.

A cloud appeared, and then another, and it began to rain. Oh boy, it poured!

"We're going to make it!" cried one wiggleskin.
"We can do it!" cheered another.

The mighty ocean was glad to welcome them back. At one time they had laughed at Edwin, but they admired him today.

And "NECKS OUT FOR ADVENTURE" is what those brave wiggleskins now say!